Spanish

SELECTED FAVORITES for GUITAR

EDITED BY HOWARD WALLACH

AN ALFRED CLASSICAL GUITAR MASTERWORK EDITION

Cover art: Alhambra from San Nicolas *(1886)*
by Henry Stanier
(British, ?-1892)
Oil on canvas
Biblioteca Provincial de Granada
PD_1923 / Wikimedia.org

Alfred Music
P.O. Box 10003
Van Nuys, CA 91410-0003
alfred.com

ISBN-10: 1-4706-1787-0
ISBN-13: 978-1-4706-1787-5

SPANISH

Contents

Preface

The first instruments truly recognizable as ancestors of the modern guitar made their appearance in Spain in the 15th century. Its popularity and the popularity of Spanish guitar music have spread since that time throughout Europe, the Americas and much of the rest of the world. This book contains some of the most popular Spanish guitar pieces, including *Malagueña*, *El Testamento de Amelia*, *Recuerdos de la Alhambra* and *Asturias-Leyenda*.

The guitar is the heart and soul of Spain, and Spain is the heart and soul of the guitar. Nobody has done more with the guitar than the Spanish. Throughout the last five centuries, the greatest number of important performers, guitar makers, and composers for the instrument have possessed Spanish surnames.

There are many reasons why so many people identify the sound of the guitar as Spanish. Perhaps it is the tuning of the guitar, with its natural notes in the first position actually outlining the Phrygian mode (E, F, G, A, B, C, D)—a sound which characterizes much Flamenco and traditional Spanish music.

The typically Spanish bass line—E, F, G, F, E—is derived from the Phrygian mode. In addition, the influence of Gypsy, Hebraic and Moorish music, along with familiar dance rhythms like the Fandango, Soleares, and Buleria, all add up to the sound we have come to identify as Spanish.

This sound has been so thoroughly ingrained in our music that we even find examples of it in jazz and rock tunes such as Joe Pass's *Paco de Lucia*, Chick Corea's *Spain*, the Doors' *Spanish Caravan*, the Eagles' *Hotel California*, and many more.

We have attempted to include in this volume only those pieces with a truly Spanish sound or character, in the belief that such music will be a joy for all.

About the Pieces in this Volume

Malagueña
A malagueña is a dance from the southern Spanish seaport of Málaga. It is in the family of the fandango, which is in triple time (usually $\frac{3}{4}$) and danced by couples to guitar and castanet accompaniment. Play with a strong steady beat at a moderate tempo.

El Testamento de Amelia
The melody of this beautiful folk ballad comes from Cataluña, an old province of northeastern Spain. It was first made famous by guitar virtuoso Miguel Llobet's ethereal setting in D Minor. In A Minor the piece conveys a simpler and more earthy beauty. Play slowly and with expression.

Estudio
Dionisio Aguado was born in Madrid in 1784, and began his guitar studies there with the renowned "Padre Dom Basilio." He became well known throughout Spain for his brilliant technique, which included the use of right-hand fingernails—unusual for that time. In 1825, Aguado moved to Paris, where he became famous as a teacher and virtuoso. This beautiful, plaintive study is from his method, *Escuela de guitarra* (Madrid, 1825). The melodic interest is all in the bass (notated with stems down).

La Llorona
The title of this traditional ballad translates as "The Weeping Woman." Though popular in Mexico, the origins of the song and its tragic tale of murder lie in Spain. Due to the freer performance style of folk songs, you may repeat any of the sections as many times as you like. Play at a moderate tempo with an ample amount of feeling.

Preludio "Endecha" & Preludio
These two highly romantic pieces by Tárrega work very well together when played as a pair. The indescribable sadness of the *Preludio "Endecha"* in D Minor is relieved by the direct and simple sweetness of the following *Preludio* in D Major. Both pieces require the 6th string to be tuned down a whole step to D.

Estudio en Mi Meno
Francisco Tárrega helped to restore the popularity of the classical guitar as a concert instrument after a period of decline in the second half of the 19th century. His many beautiful compositions in the Spanish "nationalist" style and his numerous transcriptions expanded the technical and harmonic range of the instrument. His performances on the new larger, louder, and more resonant instruments of Antonio Torres introduced the public to the potential of the modern classical guitar. Tárrega's impact as a teacher continued well into the 20th century through such students as Miguel Llobet and Emilio Pujol. Play at a lively tempo, and be sure to bring out the melody notes (the first note in each triplet) with the ring (*a*) finger.

Lágrima (Preludio)
One of Tárrega's most popular pieces, the title of this wistful little prelude means "tear" or "tear drop." Do not play too slowly, and do not let the repeated open 2nd string (B) in the accompaniment sound as loudly as the melody line (notated with stems up).

La Paloma
Sebastien de Yradier achieved considerable success as a composer of *zarzuelas*—a kind of Spanish operetta with dancing. *La Paloma* ("The Dove") has remained one of the most popular Spanish songs of the past 150 years. Play at a relaxed tempo. Tuning the 5th and 6th strings down a whole step makes the arrangement easier to play and creates a beautiful open G sound.

Romance de España
A *romance* is a lyrical and sentimental song or instrumental piece. This particular romance, by an unknown Spanish composer, first achieved great popularity when Narciso Yepes recorded it for the French film classic, *Jeux Interdits*. Be sure to bring out the melody (notated with the stems up).

Recuerdos de la Alhambra
The title, "Recollections of the Alhambra," refers to the palace built near Granada by the Moorish occupiers of Spain during the 13th and 14th centuries. One of the favorite guitar compositions of all time, it is a piece of moderate challenge, on which one should expect to work for some time to achieve mastery. Its outstanding feature is the tremolo (rapidly repeated notes) played with *a*, *m*, and *i*. Strive for an even, flowing sound, much like the fountains found at the Alhambra.

Asturias-Leyenda
The virtuoso pianist and composer Isaac Albéniz was an instrumental figure in the development of the Spanish "nationalist" school of composition. *Asturias-Leyenda* is from his "*Suite española*" which contains eight pieces for piano with both geographical and generic titles. For example, Asturias is an old province of northwestern Spain, and a *leyenda* is a type of dance.

Adelita (Mazurka)
The Spanish sound of Tárrega's compositional style is unmistakable even in his *mazurkas*—a favorite national dance of Poland. Like a number of Chopin's famous mazurkas for piano, this piece is somewhat tender and sentimental yet also a bit playful. Avoid the common mistake of playing it too slowly.

Malagueña

Traditional
Arr. H. Wallach

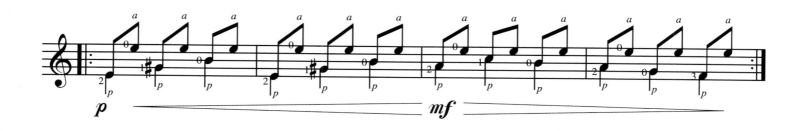

* Chords marked with a ↑ are to be strummed from bass strings to treble (towards the floor).
Chords marked with a ↓ should be strummed from treble strings to bass (towards the ceiling).

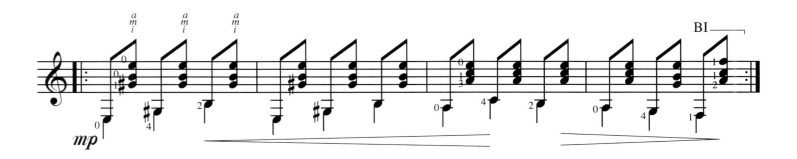

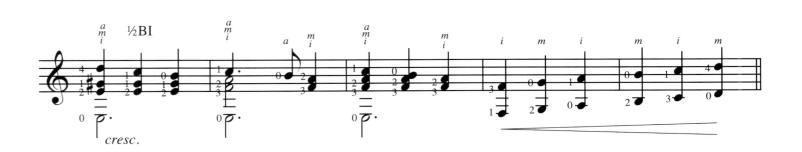

6

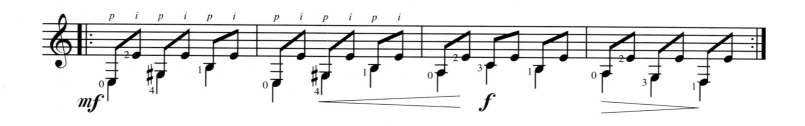

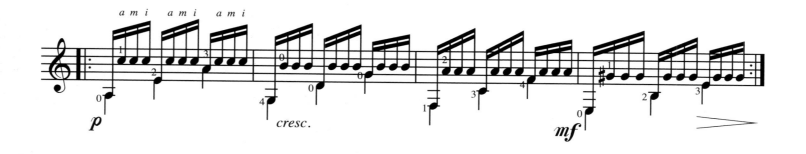

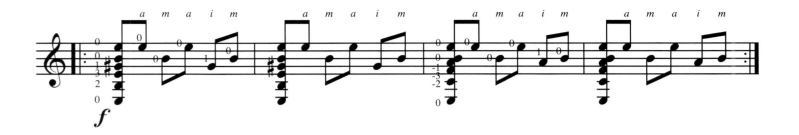

El Testamento de Amelia

Traditional
Arr. H. Wallach

Estudio

Dionisio Aguado
(1784 – 1849)

La Llorona

Traditional
Arr. H. Wallach

* Leave the 1st finger down and add the barre of beat 2.
** Keep the 1st finger down and add the barre for beat 2 only to play the C.

Preludio "Endecha"

Francisco Tárrega
(1852 – 1909)

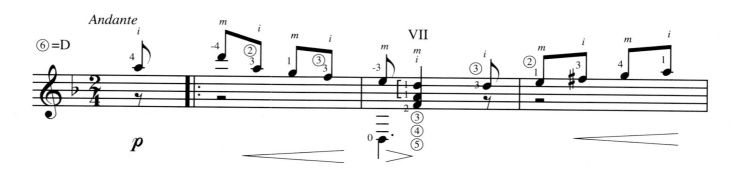

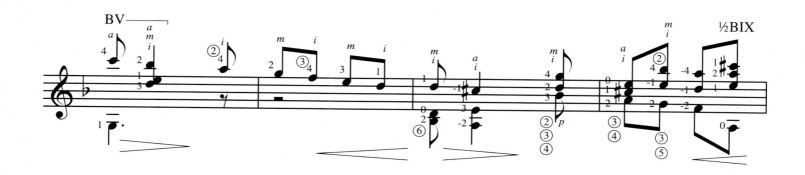

Preludio

Francisco Tárrega
(1852 – 1909)

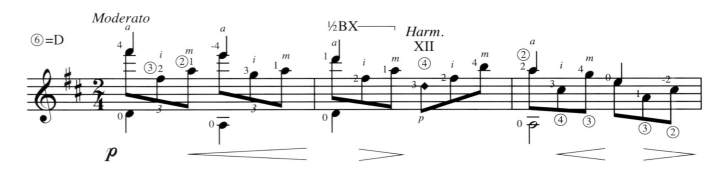

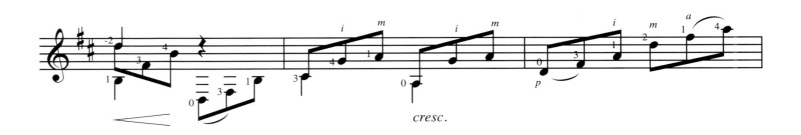

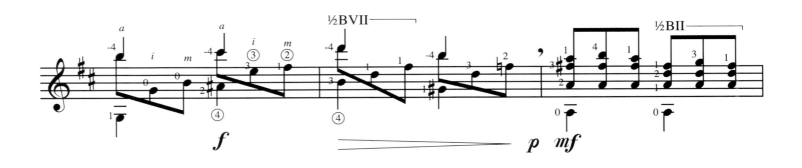

Estudio en Mi Meno

Francisco Tárrega
(1852 – 1909)

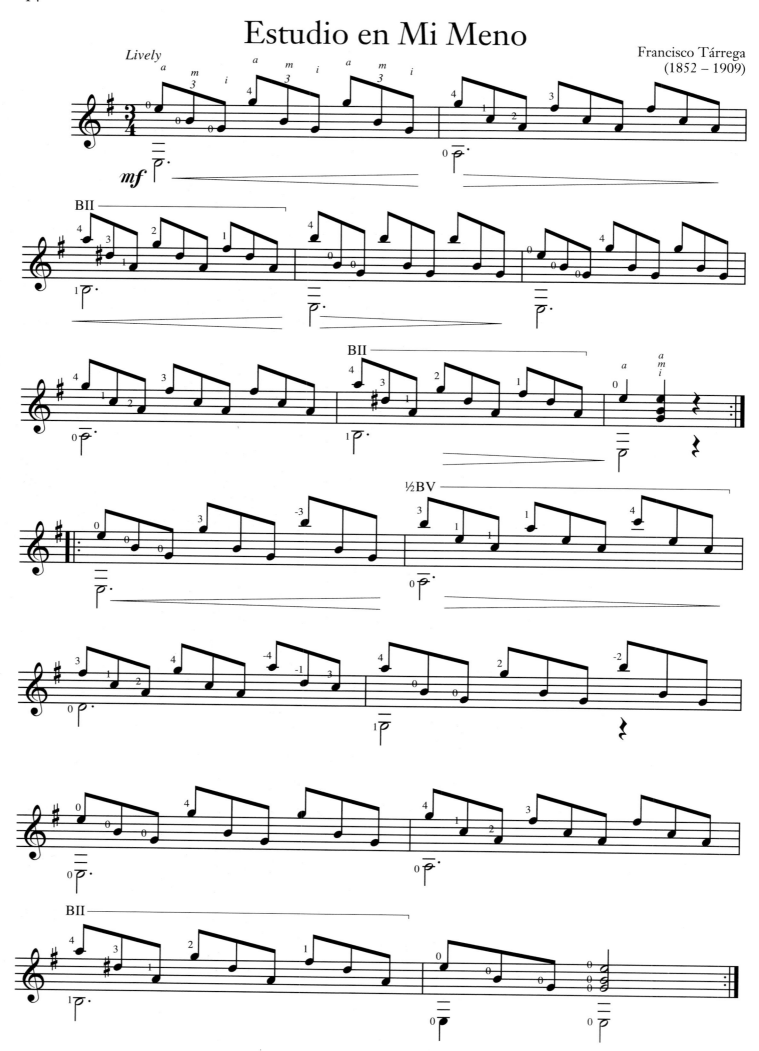

Lágrima (Preludio)

Francisco Tárrega
(1852 – 1909)

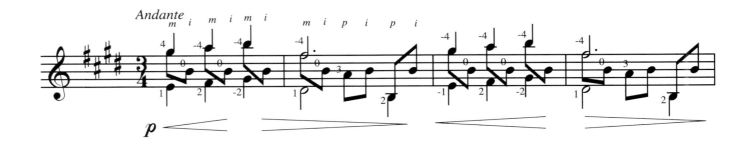

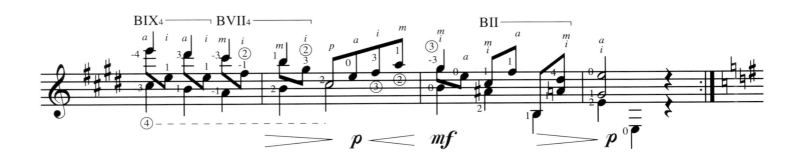

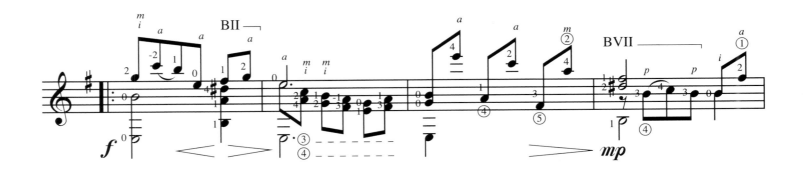

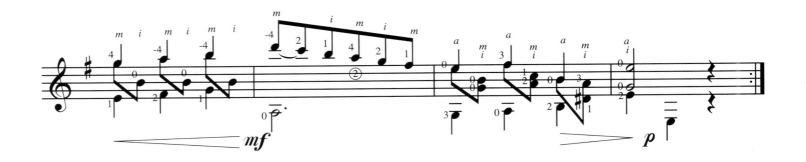

La Paloma

Sebastien de Yradier
(1809 – 1865)
Arr. H. Wallach

* Play *forte* the first time through, and *piano* the second time through.

1 x *f*
2 x *p*

Romance de España

Traditional
Arr. H. Wallach

Recuerdos de la Alhambra

Francisco Tárrega
(1852 – 1909)

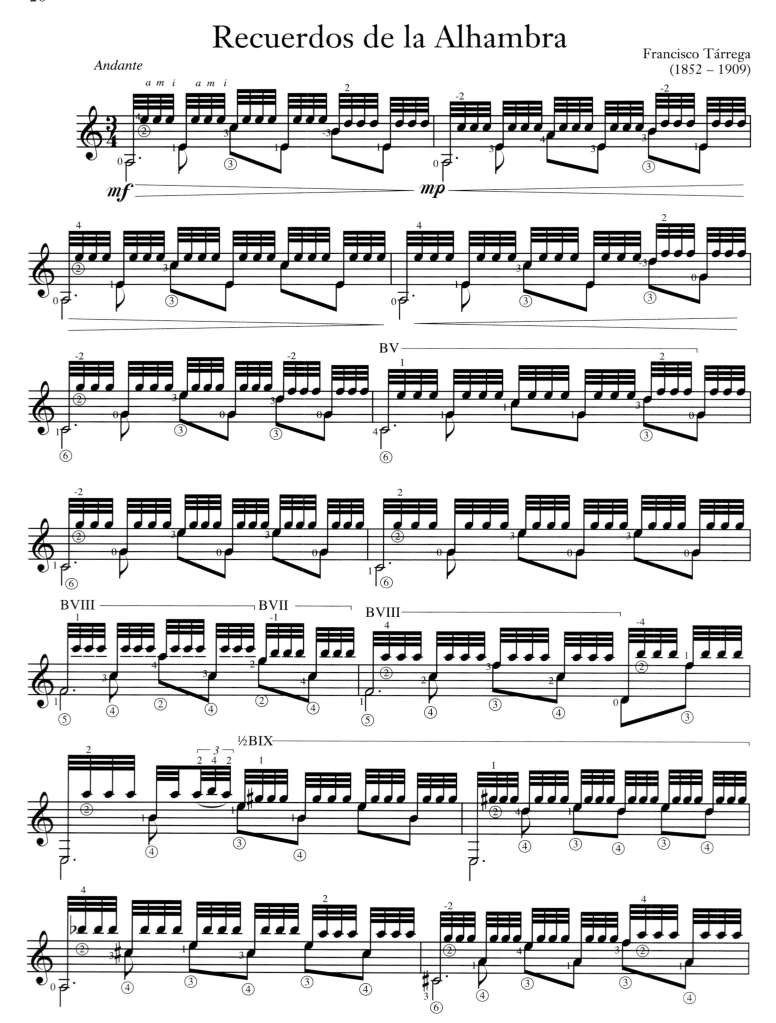

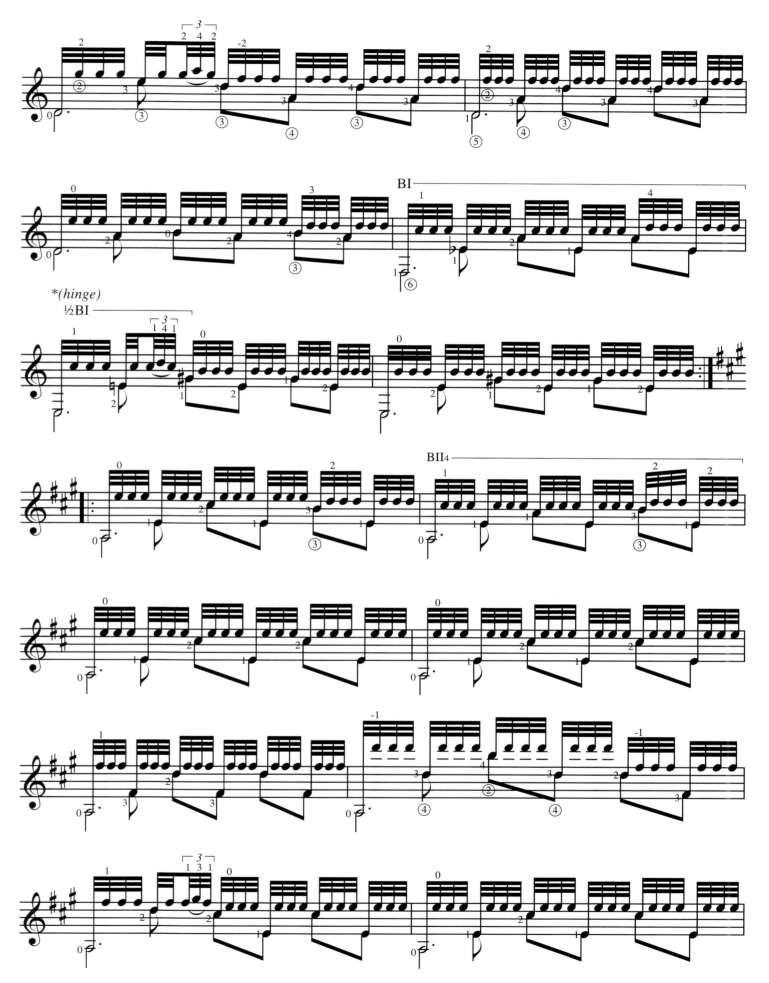

* *hinge* = Hinge barre on the 1st fret. Cover just the 2nd and 3rd strings by flattening the tip joint of your
  1st finger. As you strike the G♯ on beat 2, release the tip joint back to a normal playing position.

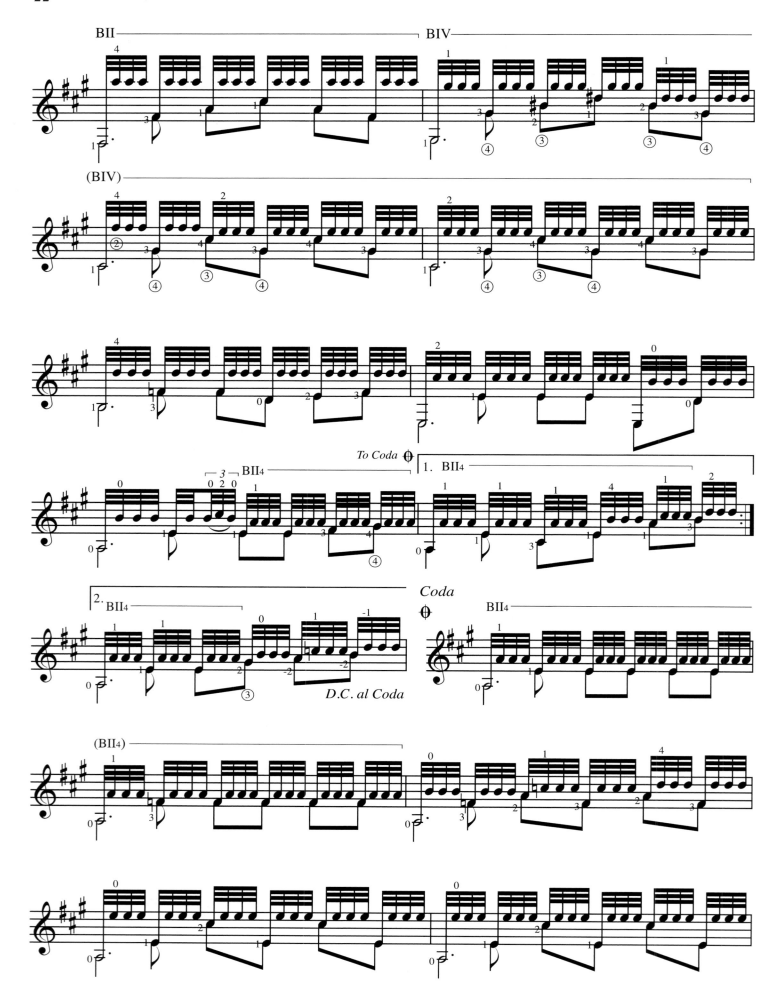

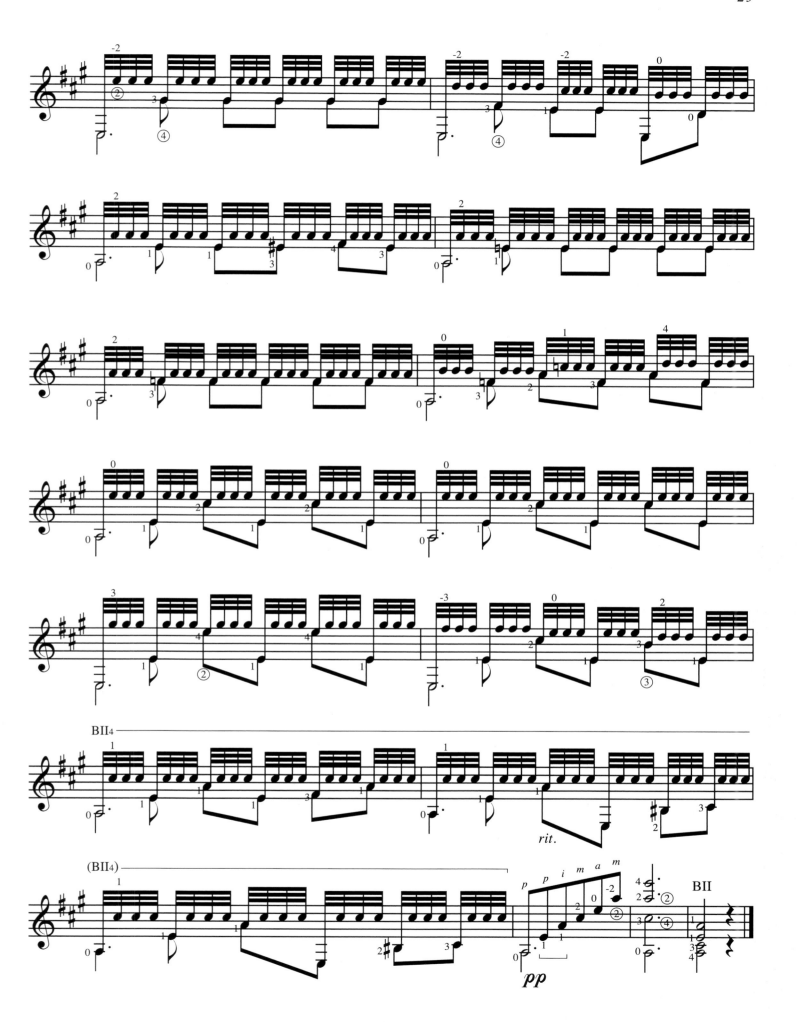

Asturias-Leyenda

Isaac Albéniz
(1860 – 1909)

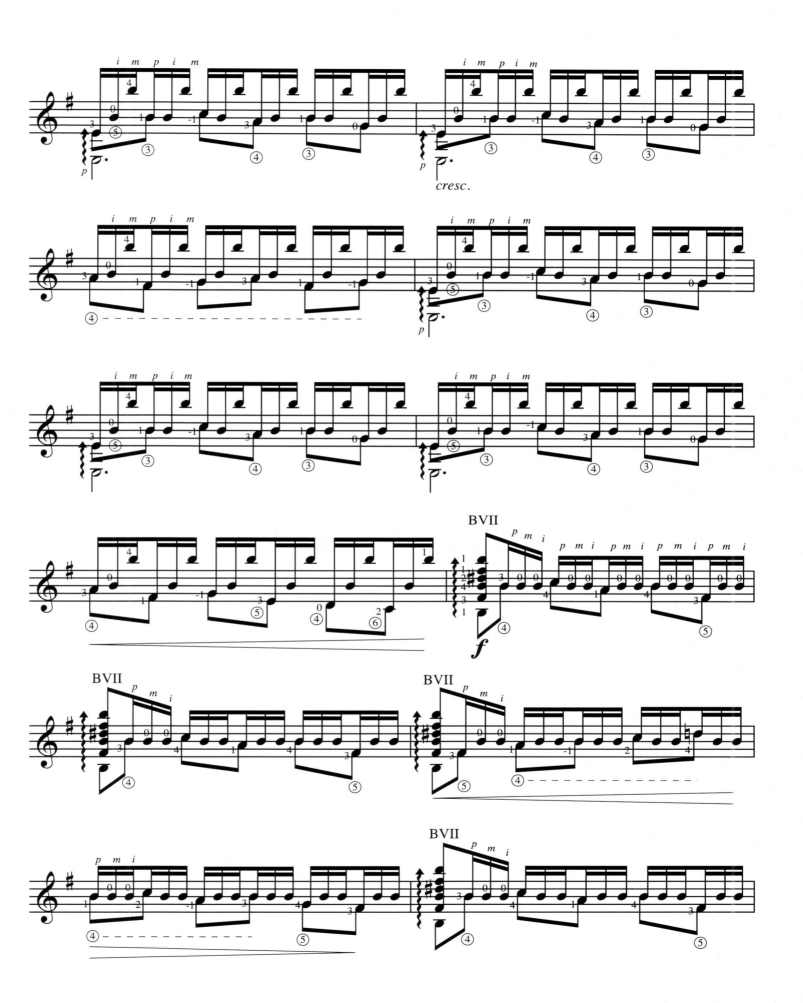

26

* The dotted slur lines are there to remind you that these pitches
  should be sustained into the chords on the following down beats.

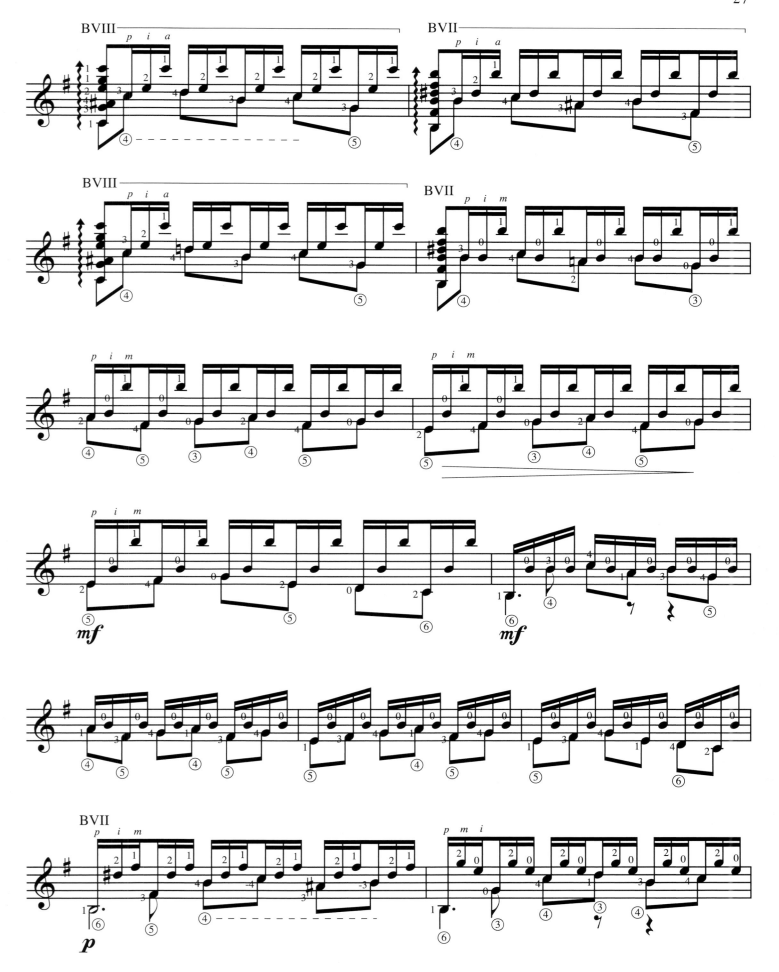

28

* Pizzicato is a muted plucking sound, emulating the plucking sound of a bowed instrument such as the violin or cello. Strings are muted with the right side of the right hand and plucked with *p*.

Adelita (Mazurka)

Francisco Tárrega
(1852 – 1909)

* This is a *glissando* mark. A glissando is a slide from one note to another. Play the 4th fret B and then, keeping your finger on the string as you slide up to the 13th fret G♯. The result will be an expressive, vocal-like gliding sound.

Signs, Symbols, and Terms

Roman Numerals		
I **1**	V **5**	IX **9**
II **2**	VI **6**	X **10**
III **3**	VII **7**	XI **11**
IV **4**	VIII **8**	XII **12**

> = **Accent**. Emphasize the note.

} = **Arpeggiate**. Quickly "roll" the chord.

∧ = **Marcato**. Emphasize more than an accent.

BV3	=	Barre three strings at the 5th fret.
BV	=	Barre all six strings at the 5th fret.
HBV	=	Hinge barre at the 5th fret. Play an individual note on the 1st string with the bottom of the 1st finger, just above the palm. Usually simplifies the next fingering.
⑥ = D	=	Tune the 6th string down to D
p, i, m, a	=	The right-hand fingers starting with the thumb.
1, 2, 3, 4, 0	=	The left-hand fingers starting with the index finger, and the open string.

adagio = A slow tempo which is faster than *largo* and slower than *andante*.

allegro = Cheerful, quick or fast.

allegretto = A lively quick tempo that moves more slowly than *allegro*.

andante = A moderate, graceful tempo, slower than *allegretto* and faster than *adagio*.

a tempo = Return to the original tempo.

cantabile = Singing.

commodo = Comfortable, leisurely.

con brio = With vigor.

con moto = With motion.

cresc. = Abbreviation for *crescendo*. Gradually becoming louder.

D.C. al Fine = *Da capo al fine.* Go back to the beginning of the piece and play to the *Fine*, which is the end of the piece.

dim. = Abbreviation for *diminuendo*. Gradually becoming softer.

dolce = Sweet.

gliss. = Abbreviation for *glissando*. To slide from one note to another. Often shown as a diagonal line with an S (slide) in guitar music.

harm. = Abbreviation for *harmonic*. Notes of the harmonic series that are very pure and clear. In this book, written at the sounding pitch with a diamond shaped note head. Touch the string lightly directly over the indicated fret and pluck, immediately removing the finger from the string.

largo = Very slow and broad.

legato = Smooth, connected.

leggiero = Light or delicate.

l.v. = Abbreviation for *laissez vibre* (let vibrate).

maestoso = Sublime or magnificent.

moderato = In a moderate tempo.

molto = Very or much.

non troppo = But not too much so.

più = More.

poco a poco = Little by little.

rall. = Abbreviation for *rallentando*. Becoming gradually slower.

rit. = Abbreviation for *ritardando*. Becoming gradually slower.

sempre = Always.

sostenuto = Sustained.

staccato = Short, detached.

tranquillo = Tranquil, calm, quiet.

vivace = Lively, quick.

ALFRED CLASSICAL GUITAR MASTERWORK EDITIONS
Light Classics Arrangements for Guitar

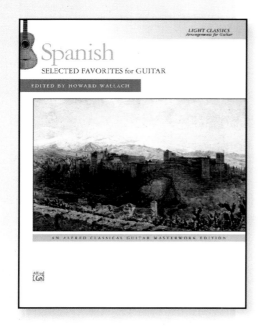

Familiar favorites for classical guitar.

SPANISH

EDITED BY HOWARD WALLACH

Intended for both working guitarists and those who play strictly for the enjoyment of great music, this collection of Spanish favorites for guitar will add something special to any party or social gathering. Including such popular pieces as "Malagueña," "Asturias (Leyenda)," Francisco Tárrega's "Recuerdos de la Alhambra," "Lágrima," and the famous E minor "Romance de España," this edition will provide you with a repertoire of crowd-pleasers for any event.

Go to alfred.com/classicalguitar to see more Light Classics editions.

43653 $9.99 in USA

ISBN 1-4706-1787-0

alfred.com

ISBN-10: 1-4706-1787-0
ISBN-13: 978-1-4706-1787-5

PRINTED IN THE USA

SOR
SELECTED WORKS for GUITAR

EDITED AND FINGERED BY MARC TEICHOLZ

AN ALFRED CLASSICAL GUITAR MASTERWORK EDITION

Alfred